D1455698

Copyright © 1985 Parker Brothers, Division of CPG Products Corp. All rights reserved. Published in the United States by Parker Brothers, Division of CPG Products Corp.

HUGGA BUNCH is a trademark of Hallmark Cards Inc., used under license.
HUGGA BUNCH designs © 1985 Hallmark Cards Incorporated. All rights reserved.

Library of Congress Cataloging in Publication Data: Anderson, Janet, 1946 — A hug for a new friend.
SUMMARY: Anxious about her new babysitter, Sarah visits Huggaland and learns that "Hugs make friends and friends make hugs."
1. Childrens' stories, American.
[1. Hugging — Fiction. 2. Friendship — Fiction. 3. Baby sitters — Fiction]
I. Lipking, Ronald, ill.   II. Title.
PZ7.A5365Hu   1985   [E]   85-5673   ISBN 0-910313-91-1
Manufactured in the United States of America   1 2 3 4 5 6 7 8 9 0   -01

PROOF OF PURCHASE
A Hug for a New Friend.
H.B.

HUGGA BUNCH™

A Hug for a New Friend

Story by Janet Anderson
Pictures by Ron C. Lipking

It was bedtime on Sunday night, and Sarah's mother was ready to tuck her in. Sarah turned a perfect back somersault into her room and then climbed into bed. She yawned sleepily.

"I can't wait to see Kim after play school tomorrow," Sarah said. "I want to show her my back somersault."

"Your back somersault is wonderful," said her mother. "But I'm afraid Kim won't be able to see it for a while. She called just after dinner while you were reading with Daddy. She has a terrible cold; she could hardly talk. It will be at least a week until she's better."

"A week!" said Sarah. "Then who's going to stay with me until you get home from work?"

"I've already called a very nice girl who's agreed to babysit with you until Kim is better. Her name is…"

"I don't want to know her name," said Sarah. "I don't like her. I want Kim to stay with me."

"But Sarah, you haven't even met her. Laura sounded very kind on the phone. I'm sure you'll like her when you get to know her."

Sarah shook her head. She was trying not to cry. "She's probably eight feet tall and has mean little eyes. I want Kim!"

Her mother patted her back. "You'll feel better about it in the morning. Laura's going to join us for breakfast so you can meet her while I'm still here. Now, give me a hug and sleep tight."

But Sarah felt so awful she couldn't hug back. This one-way hug made Sarah's mother feel very sad, and the smile quickly faded from her face.

It took a long time for Sarah to fall asleep. When she did, she dreamed about a babysitter with a frowning face. "I hate back somersaults," the babysitter kept saying. "Back somersaults are silly."

"They are not silly," Sarah cried, and then woke up.

It was very early. The sun was just beginning to spill light into her room. But it wasn't the light that woke her. It was a giggle. A giggle? Sarah sat up in bed. Then she heard it again. It was a lighthearted sound, and very happy.

Where was it coming from? Sarah looked around
her room, and there, poking its head through the
mirror on her door, was the cutest, friendliest-looking
little creature she had ever seen.

"Who are you?" said Sarah. With another happy giggle, the little person turned a cartwheel and landed right in Sarah's lap. Then she gave Sarah such a warm tickly hug that Sarah had to giggle, too. "But who are you?" she repeated.

"Guess what?" said the little person. "I'm one of the Hugga Bunch, but we're not all the same. See if you're able to come up with my name. I do what I am, and I am what I do." She gave Sarah a second, fast tickly hug and turned another cartwheel onto the floor. "I like to hug *new* friends, how about you?"

"Me?" said Sarah. "I...I don't know." She was remembering the new babysitter who was going to be there for breakfast. She certainly wouldn't want to hug *her*.

"Guess what?" said the little person, twirling around and landing in a funny heap. "A hug's so much fun, I'm sure you'll agree. A hug makes a new friend an *old* friend; you'll see. But now for my name — are you still in a pickle? I am what I do. What I do best is…"

Sarah found herself being given another funny, happy hug that was half a hug and half a…"Tickle!" she shouted. "Your name must be Tickle!"

"Guess what?" said the little person. "You're bright! You're right! I'm Tickles, you're Sarah; how do you do? And now please meet Gigglet; she'll be a friend, too."

Now, for the first time, Sarah saw that someone was clinging to Tickles' shoulder. She was so little with such a warm, funny smile, it made Sarah laugh just to look at her.

Tickles clapped her hands. "Guess what? You're laughing. That's great and I'm glad. Last night when we saw you, you looked very sad."

Sarah's smile faded and she nodded. "My babysitter is sick, and I've got to have a new one for a whole week. I know I won't like her and…"

"Guess what?" Tickles interrupted. "*Won't* is sad. *Will* is more fun. The Huggas will show you how it's done. Close your eyes. Hold my hand. We're off to visit Huggaland!"

Tickles led Sarah to the mirror and gave her a big hug. To Sarah's amazement, her mirror began turning all soft and fluffy, as if it were being hugged by a cloud.

Sarah wasn't sure she liked this. Where was Tickles taking her? What if she didn't like the Hugga Bunch? What if they didn't like her? But it was too late. Tickles had led her right through the mirror.

Stretching out before her were rolling hills made of softly colored patches, and beautiful big trees that were as fluffy as cotton candy. Little plush houses dotted this wonderfully soft landscape.

"Welcome to Huggaland," said a tiny voice. All around her, Sarah could hear giggles and gentle friendly voices. Then, in twos and threes, all the Huggas crept out from their hiding places and began to gather around Sarah and Tickles.

Sarah blinked her eyes. She had never seen so
many warm smiles, so many happy faces. "Guess
what?" she heard Tickles say. "These are my friends.
They're your friends, too. They hope that you'll like
them; they really like you."

"But they don't even know me," said Sarah.
"How can they like me if they don't even know me?"

She felt herself being wrapped in a loving, tender hug, and the voice that spoke was warm and strong. "I'm Huggins," the voice said. "I can like you, because I know that if I'm friendly to you, you'll feel good and be friendly to me. And feeling friendly is what hugs are all about. Why, hugs make friends and then friends…friends make hugs!"

"That's right," said a small, cheery Hugga as she came scurrying down the hill. On one hand, she was balancing a tray of round little cups filled with pink lemonade that she'd made for Sarah and the others. But just as the little Hugga reached the bottom of the hill, the tray slipped out of her hand and crashed to the ground. Lemonade spilled everywhere!

"Oh my!" Sarah cried.

"Oh poor Patooty!" Huggins said.

Patooty quickly bent down and began picking up
the empty cups. But even in her rush, she couldn't
hide her sadness.

"Wish someone would hug her happy,"
Huggins said.

"Oh," said Sarah, forgetting everything but the unhappy little person before her. She even forgot to be shy or to worry if Patooty would like her. She ran over and knelt down. "Don't be sad," she said. "I like you." Without thinking, she gave Patooty a big, warm, friendly hug.

Patooty hugged her back. Patooty's hug was as soft and as warm as cotton, and Sarah had never felt so happy. Was making new friends as simple as this?

Huggins seemed to read her thoughts. "It's as simple as that," she said. "Remember: Making new friends is easy and fun, just give them a hug and your friendship's begun."

"'Just give them a hug and your friendship's begun,'" repeated Sarah. She closed her eyes to remember it better, and from far away she heard her mother calling. She ran toward the sound and suddenly she was back in her room. Sarah opened her door.

"Is she here?" she said. "Is Laura here?"
Her mother looked worried. "Yes," she said. "She looks very nice. Please try and like her, Sarah."

Sarah didn't answer. Instead, she ran down the hall and into the kitchen. A girl was talking to her father. The girl was very tall, and for a minute, Sarah felt awkward. She looked up into her eyes. Would they be little and mean? The girl looked down at her, and her eyes were large and brown and …
"Why," thought Sarah, "she may be shy and a little scared, too!"

She heard a soft little giggle, and out of the
corner of her eye saw two small faces peeking out of
the mirror by the door. Tickles was laughing and
Huggins was smiling her warm smile. "Just give them
a hug and your friendship's begun," came the whisper,
and then the two faces disappeared. Sarah nodded
and turned back to Laura.

"Hello" she said. "I'm Sarah and you're Laura. Can I give you a hug?"

Laura's face lit up. "You certainly can," she said. She leaned down and Sarah gave her the softest and warmest hug she could. "Hugs make friends and friends make hugs. Did you know that?" Sarah asked.

"I do now," said Laura and hugged her back. "And now that we're going to be good friends, can you do something for me? I don't know how to turn a back somersault, and I heard you turn the best ones in town. Can you show me how?"

Laughing, Sarah turned three perfect back somersaults toward the breakfast table. She hugged her mother and her father, and then she hugged Laura. The hug for Laura was the biggest and the best of all, because it was a hug for a new friend.